SCIENCE DISCOVERY

Crime

Q&A

Janice Parker

www.av2books.com

AV² provides enriched content that supplements and complements this book. Weigl's AV² books strive to create inspired learning and engage young minds in a total learning experience.

Your AV² Media Enhanced books come alive with...

 Audio
Listen to sections of the book read aloud.

 Key Words
Study vocabulary, and complete a matching word activity.

 Video
Watch informative video clips.

 Quizzes
Test your knowledge.

 Embedded Weblinks
Gain additional information for research.

 Slide Show
View images and captions, and prepare a presentation.

 Try This!
Complete activities and hands-on experiments.

... and much, much more!

Go to **www.av2books.com,** and enter this book's unique code.

BOOK CODE

N442361

AV² by Weigl brings you media enhanced books that support active learning.

Published by AV² by Weigl
350 5ᵗʰ Avenue, 59ᵗʰ Floor
New York, NY 10118
Websites: www.av2books.com   www.weigl.com

Library of Congress Control Number: 2013953132

ISBN 978-1-4896-0684-6 (hardcover)
ISBN 978-1-4896-0685-3 (softcover)
ISBN 978-1-4896-0686-0 (single-user eBook)
ISBN 978-1-4896-0687-7 (multi-user eBook)

Printed in the United States of America, in North Mankato, Minnesota
1 2 3 4 5 6 7 8 9 18 17 16 15 14

042014
WEP301113

Project Coordinator Aaron Carr
Designer Mandy Christiansen

Every reasonable effort has been made to trace ownership and to obtain permission to reprint copyright material. The publishers would be pleased to have any errors or omissions brought to their attention so that they may be corrected in subsequent printings.

Photo Credits
Weigl acknowledges Getty Images as its primary photo supplier for this title.

Contents

What Is a Crime?

Any action that is against the law can be called a crime. Every society in the world has crime. Wherever there are people, there are crimes. Science plays an important role in dealing with crime. With the help of science, we can prevent many crimes from happening, as well as solve crimes already committed. If a crime occurs, science helps police investigate it. Science also helps them understand how the crime took place, catch criminal suspects, and make sure that a court jury is convinced of a suspect's guilt.

To fully understand a crime, scientists and police have to ask questions. They will ask questions such as who might have done it, are there any victims, and is there any **evidence**. By thinking about the problem and asking questions, scientists and police can gain a better understanding of the crime.

How Scientists Use Inquiry to Answer Questions

When scientists try to answer a question, they follow the process of scientific inquiry. They begin by making observations and asking questions. Then, they propose an answer to the question. This is called the hypothesis. The hypothesis guides scientists as they research the issue. Research can involve performing experiments or reading books on the subject. When the research is finished, scientists examine the results and review their hypothesis. Often, they discover that the hypothesis was incorrect. If this happens, they revise their hypothesis and go through the process of scientific inquiry again.

Process of Scientific Inquiry

Observation

There are many different types of crimes and many ways to prevent and solve them. So what exactly is a crime?

Have You Answered the Question?

The cycle of scientific inquiry never truly ends. For example, once you know how genetic material in blood can identify suspects, you may need to ask, "What other types of evidence contain genetic material?"

Research

Scientists have studied crimes, how they occur, and how best to solve them. They do this by asking questions such as, "How can we identify a suspect based on blood found at the crime scene?"

Results

Finding genetic material at a crime scene allows investigators to identify a suspect with almost 100-percent certainty. Discovering how genetic material can help solve crimes leads to more questions, more hypotheses, and more experiments.

Hypothesis

Investigators can narrow down a list of suspects based on blood type, but blood type alone cannot identify a specific criminal. That has led scientists to wonder whether **genetic material** in blood might offer more certain evidence.

Experiment

To test this hypothesis, scientists perform experiments comparing genetic material in blood found at crime scenes with the genetic material of possible suspects.

What Is a Crime Scene?

A crime scene is the location where a crime took place. The first step in investigating a crime is often to visit the crime scene. Examples of crime scenes are buildings that burglars have broken into or the place where someone has found an injured or dead person. If the scene for a murder is a home, the crime scene includes the room where the body was found as well as the rest of the house. Police search the entire area for clues that may help them solve the crime.

Police block off crime scenes so that the evidence is not disturbed. Even the most careful criminals usually leave behind clues. Before the evidence is collected, police take photographs of the area. Then, they collect anything that could be a clue to the crime. Police wear plastic gloves when collecting a piece of evidence so that they do not leave their own fingerprints on the object. They place and label all evidence in separate plastic bags. Investigators change their gloves often so that they do not move tiny bits from one piece of evidence to another. After investigators collect all the evidence, they take it to a police laboratory for analysis. Police use this evidence to answer questions about the crime. These activities are called crime scene investigation.

> All evidence is important, from a single strand of hair to a bullet after it has been fired.

Digging Deeper

Your Challenge!

In some crimes, such as kidnapping, police may not know where the crime took place, so they cannot start by searching the crime scene. To dig deeper into the issue:

Research a famous kidnapping case from history. How did clues from the crime scene help the police figure out what happened?

Summary

A crime scene is where someone committed a crime. Police search the crime scene for evidence, such as fingerprints, to answer questions about what happened.

Further Inquiry

Police may find weapons at a crime scene. Maybe we should ask:

How do police know which gun was used in a crime?

How Do Police Know Which Gun Was Used in a Crime?

If police find a weapon near a crime scene, they need to find out whether it was used to commit the crime. Police look at the bullets found in the victim's body or at the crime scene. The study of guns and bullets in criminal investigations is called ballistics. An unused bullet is smooth on the outside. When fired from a gun, the bullet gets scratched as it moves through the barrel of the gun. The barrel leaves unique lines and ridges on the bullet. Bullets fired from the same gun have the same ridges.

❯ Studying a bullet hole can help investigators determine from where the gun was fired.

If police find a gun they think may have been used in a crime, they will test fire some bullets from that gun. Then, they closely examine the bullets. If the ridges on the bullets match those on the bullet found at the crime scene, police confirm that the gun was used for the crime. To determine whether two bullets at a crime scene were fired from the same gun, police examine the bullets, looking for scratches made by the barrel of the gun. If both bullets have the same scratches, police know they were fired from the same gun.

⌄ Police can sometimes identify a suspect based on fingerprints left behind on the murder weapon.

How Do Scientists Know the Cause of Death?

An autopsy is the detailed study of the body of the victim. Experts often perform an autopsy when someone dies, especially if the death occurs in suspicious circumstances. Usually, an autopsy can help tell how and when a person died. **Forensic pathologists** do autopsies in medical laboratories. To do an autopsy, a pathologist first looks closely at the body of the dead person. The pathologist photographs and describes in writing any bruises, wounds, or marks. If there are gunshot wounds, the pathologist can help determine what type of gun was used and how close the gun was to the victim when it was fired. The pathologist removes any pieces of bullet from the body.

If there are knife wounds, the pathologist counts the wounds and can even determine by the placement of the wound whether the killer is right-handed or left-handed. Bruise marks around the neck often mean that the victim was strangled. The bruises are sometimes measured to determine the size of the killer's hands.

After examining the outside of the body, the pathologist cuts the body open. The pathologist removes and weighs the organs. Then, the expert examines any food in the stomach, which might provide useful clues about what the person did in the last hours of life. At this point, scientists also test body fluids to check for the presence of poisons.

❯ Pathologists use surgical tools to study dead bodies.

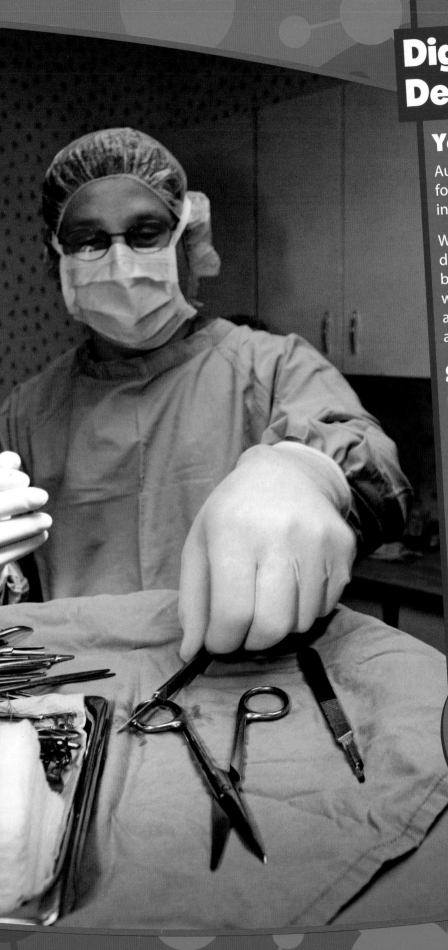

Digging Deeper

Your Challenge!

Autopsies are not performed for every death. To dig deeper into the issue:

Write down what kind of deaths might be followed by an autopsy. Research when the law requires an autopsy. How do the answers compare?

Summary

Pathologists perform an autopsy to help figure out how a person died. They may be able to tell whether the criminal was right-handed or left-handed.

Further Inquiry

Studying a dead body can also help tell when the crime was committed. Maybe we should ask:

How do scientists determine the time of death?

How Do Scientists Determine the Time of Death?

When investigating a murder case, pathologists must try to figure out exactly when the victim died. This information helps narrow down suspects. To estimate the time of death, pathologists look for various pointers. After death, body temperature steadily cools down until it is the same as the temperature of the surrounding area. By understanding how fast a body cools down under different conditions, scientists can roughly estimate the time of death.

Another factor investigators use to find the time of death is lividity. This refers to the color of areas on a dead body that darken after death. Gravity causes blood in a victim's body to settle in the areas that are closest to the ground. Lividity usually occurs half an hour to three hours after a person's death. Scientists can tell that a body was moved after that time if the dark marks are not close to the ground.

About three to five hours after death, the muscles in a body usually become stiff. This condition is known as rigor mortis. Rigor mortis disappears about 24 to 36 hours after death. If rigor mortis is present in a victim, scientists know that the death happened in the previous day and a half.

Decomposition is the breakdown of **cells** in a plant or animal that is no longer alive. This begins immediately after death. Scientists are often able to estimate the time of death by looking at how much decomposition has taken place. **Bacteria** and **fungi** that cannot survive on a living **organism** cause decomposition. They make the body change color and produce odors.

Insects cause decomposition by laying eggs on the body. When the eggs hatch, the **larvae** feed on the skin and tissues. Various insects lay their eggs at different times. Some insects lay their eggs soon after a person has died. Others will not lay their eggs until a body has been dead for months.

In addition, all insects have life cycles. Many insects, for example, begin their lives as eggs, hatch into larvae, and then change into their adult form. By determining the insects' stage of life, scientists can estimate how long a person has been dead.

Your Challenge!

Pathologists can sometimes figure out time of death by studying insects on the dead body. To dig deeper into the issue:

Research the life cycle of a blue bottle fly. About how long might the person have been dead if the insects are in the larvae stage?

Summary

To determine time of death, experts study the temperature, lividity, stiffness, and decomposition of the body. They also look for insects.

Further Inquiry

Not all crimes involve murder. Some criminals use fake money. Maybe we should ask:

How do investigators identify forgeries and counterfeits?

↖ The female blue bottle fly often lays her eggs in dead animals. Blue bottle fly eggs hatch into maggots that immediately begin to eat dead flesh, causing it to decompose.

How Do Investigators Identify Forgeries and Counterfeits?

Forgeries, or fakes, are copies of an object. Criminals produce them to trick people into believing that an item is genuine. **Forgers** are known to make copies of famous paintings, jewelry, and important documents, such as a passport or a **will**. Criminals sometimes also forge a signature on a check or credit card receipt to steal money or merchandise.

Scientists use many different methods to find out whether something is genuine or a forgery. Most artists have a way of painting or drawing that makes their work unique and difficult to copy. Paints and other materials that are used today are different from those used many years ago. By analyzing the chemicals in a painting, scientists can often tell whether the painting is real.

People also make fake, or counterfeit, money. New technologies, such as color laser printers, make it easier for criminals to make counterfeit paper money. Most countries add details to their money to make it more difficult to copy.

⌄ Some criminals try to pass off cheap watches as more expensive brands.

> Fake U.S. $20 bills do not have ink that changes from copper to green, a security thread, and a watermark, or faint image, visible on both sides.

Investigators look for these special features when they are trying to find out whether money is genuine or counterfeit. For example, some bills now have small **holograms** that cannot be copied easily. Most bills also have words written on them in very small letters. These tiny words are very difficult to copy. Another way to identify counterfeit money is to test the paper and ink. Counterfeiters cannot easily get the same materials that are used to make real money.

Digging Deeper

Your Challenge!

Criminals sometimes fake signatures. With careful examination, police can spot forgeries. To dig deeper into the issue:

Experiment with a friend by trying to copy each other's signatures. See whether a third person can identify which signatures are forgeries. What does that person look for?

Summary

Some criminals create forgeries of artwork, jewelry, and money to trick others. Police study details, such as paint type or small writing on currency, to identify fakes.

Further Inquiry

Scientists can study a signature to determine whether it is fake. Maybe we should ask:

What can scientists tell from a piece of writing?

What Can Scientists Tell from a Piece of Writing?

Every person's handwriting is unique. Police analyze handwriting to learn more about a crime. By comparing several different pieces of writing, they can often decide who wrote a letter asking for **ransom** or forged a name on a check. The study of handwriting is called graphology.

Handwriting experts, or graphologists, are trained to spot differences between people's handwriting. Even though handwriting can change depending on a person's mood or how quickly a person writes, certain details about the writing stay the same. People with certain mental illnesses sometimes have a specific type of handwriting. If someone is receiving threatening letters from an unknown person, a graphologist can look at the writing and help determine whether the person writing the letters is dangerous. A graphologist may also be able to look at a letter and know whether the writer was lying or telling the truth.

❮ Handwriting experts examine the curve, slant, and size of each letter to help determine who the writer was.

Digging Deeper

Your Challenge!

After learning to write at school, people develop unique handwriting features. To dig deeper into the issue:

Find a letter or essay you wrote a few years ago. Compare it to something you wrote recently. How does your handwriting on both documents differ? Is it obvious that you wrote both?

Summary

Graphologists can help solve crimes by analyzing handwriting. Each person's handwriting has unique **traits**. Experts are able to use those traits to identify criminals who have committed forgeries.

Further Inquiry

Handwriting is not the only clue left behind at crime scenes. Maybe we should ask:

How do cloth fibers help police investigate crimes?

∧ In some criminal cases, handwriting samples are damaged or incomplete.

How Do Cloth Fibers Help Police Investigate Crimes?

As people move, tiny fibers fall from their clothing. These fibers float in the air and attach themselves to other objects or people. If a person sits in a car, his or her clothes are likely to leave behind fibers on the seats or the floor. These tiny fibers can help link a suspect to a crime.

⌄ A powerful microscope helps scientists find evidence that may be difficult to see without any special tools.

↑ Using a microscope, scientists may be able to discover details about a pair of jeans left by a suspect.

Fibers are usually difficult to see without a magnifying glass or a powerful microscope. Police often use tape to collect fibers from a crime scene or a suspect's clothes. The fibers are taken to a police lab and examined under a microscope. Fibers that look similar to the human eye look very different under a microscope. Microscopes make it easy to identify wool, cotton, nylon, polyester, and other types of fibers. Bumps and ridges often show up on the strands. If fibers found in two different places look the same, they are analyzed chemically to tell whether they may have come from the same source.

The types of fibers found in some clothing, such as blue jeans, are common. These fibers may be less useful to police because they are found nearly everywhere. Other fibers, however, are very rare. They may have been produced years ago or made only in one country. They may have an unusual dye color. Police try to trace manufacturers to find out what companies may have bought products made with these fibers.

Your Challenge!

Fibers that appear similar may look very different when magnified. To dig deeper into the issue:

Experiment by using pieces of tape to remove a single fiber from several cloth items. Tape the fibers to a piece of white paper. Examine each fiber with a magnifying glass. Can you tell which item each fiber came from?

Summary

Scientists study clothing fibers from crime scenes to help identify suspects. Scientists may be able to tell where or when the clothing was made or sold.

Further Inquiry

Fibers may not be enough to solve a crime. Maybe we should ask:

How do police use photography to investigate crimes?

How Do Police Use Photography to Investigate Crimes?

At a crime scene, police photographers take many pictures to use as evidence. They shoot images of the entire crime scene and close-ups of any victims. A photographer also records images of evidence such as blood stains, footprints, and tire tracks. Photographs from a crime scene help remind investigators about some of the details they may have forgotten or not noticed at the time. Photographs may also be used in court to help prove the guilt or innocence of a suspect.

Some of the collected evidence, such as a piece of clothing, will be photographed again later at the police laboratory. This kind of evidence needs to be examined more closely under a microscope. A photograph of a microscope image is called a photomicrograph.

Police photographers also take photos of anyone who has been arrested. These photographs are called mug shots. If a criminal escapes from jail, police sometimes publish mug shots in newspapers and on websites or show them on television. Someone reading news or watching television may recognize the person and provide information to help police catch the criminal.

> ❯ Digital cameras allow police photographers to review images at the crime scene. This helps them make sure they have clear pictures of all the evidence.

Digging Deeper

Your Challenge!

Police photographers take pictures at crime scenes. Sometimes people taking photos or videos of something else capture footage of a crime without knowing it. To dig deeper into the issue:

Hypothesize how those photos or videos might affect the investigation. Might a bystander capture something that the police missed?

Summary

Police photographers take photographs of crime scenes, including blood stains, footprints and tire tracks. The photographs can be used as evidence.

Further Inquiry

Photographs of footprints from a crime scene are evidence. Maybe we should ask:

How does dirt help solve crimes?

How Does Dirt Help Solve Crimes?

Plants and dirt can help police to link a suspect to a crime scene. To many people, most dirt looks the same. However, dirt from different areas contains different things. A scientist looking at dirt under a microscope may be able to tell where it came from. If dirt found on a suspect's shoes or in the treads of a car tire matches the dirt found at a crime scene, police try to prove that the suspect was at the crime scene. Dirt is also useful for showing footprints or tire tracks.

If footprints are found at a crime scene, investigators photograph the prints and make a plaster cast of them. At the police laboratory, scientists can determine that the prints came from a certain make and size of shoe. They can estimate how much the person weighs by how deep the imprints are in the ground. The design and depth of car tire tracks can sometimes help police figure out the type of car the suspect drove.

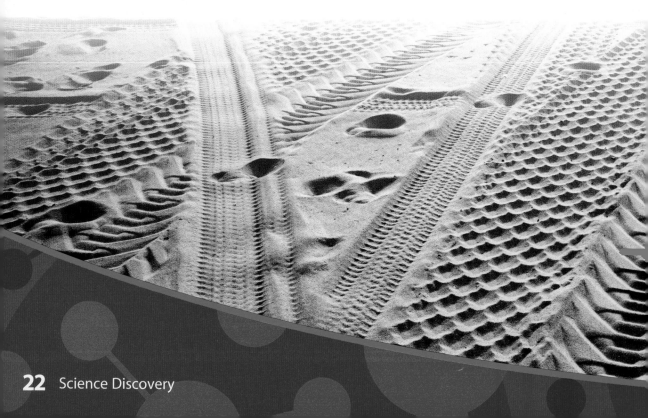

> Dirt in shoe soles may contain things such as seeds or grains of sand that can help determine where a crime took place.

Plants also help investigators. For example, **pollen** is found in most flowering plants. As people walk past plants, pollen sticks to their clothing or shoes. Different places have different types of pollen. If there is pollen on the clothing of a victim or suspect, or if pollen is found at the crime scene, police may be able to use that information to help solve the crime.

⌄ Investigators can sometimes determine the brand of a tire based on tread marks.

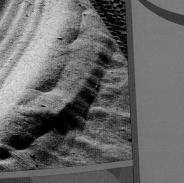

Digging Deeper

Your Challenge!

Tire tracks can provide information about the car that made them. To dig deeper into the issue:

Experiment by riding your bike through soft ground. Examine the tire tread pattern you leave behind. How does it change if the tires are not fully inflated?

Summary

Investigators dig into dirt at crime scenes to find evidence. Footprints, tire treads, and pollen can give clues.

Further Inquiry

In some cases, police have more than just evidence. They have a suspect to question. Maybe we should ask:

How can police tell if a suspect is lying?

Q&A

How Can Police Tell If a Suspect Is Lying?

Scientists invented a lie detector machine, also known as a polygraph machine. It keeps track of the internal body changes that occur when someone is lying. Polygraph machines may help police decide whether someone is telling the truth.

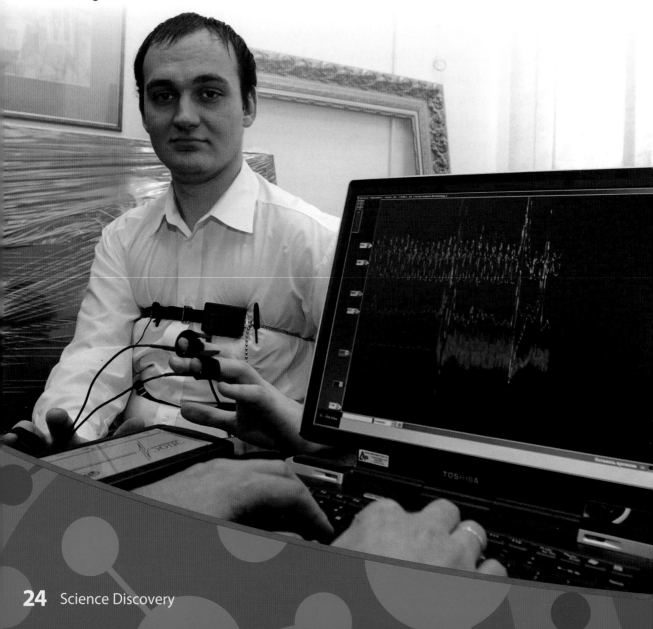

People are often raised to believe that it is wrong to lie. They usually feel guilty when they do not tell the truth. When people lie, their body language often gives the truth away. They turn their eyes away and start to fidget. Many things also happen inside their bodies when they lie. For example, a person may start to sweat, and his or her heart may beat faster.

A polygraph machine measures breathing rate, pulse rate, blood pressure, and sweat production. To analyze someone, a person is connected to the polygraph and asked several questions. If the person lies when answering some of the questions, the machine detects changes in pulse rate and other body functions.

Although polygraphs are useful to police, they are not perfect. Some people are able to lie without any physical changes. Others are so nervous that physical changes make it look as though they are lying even when they are telling the truth. In some countries, the results of lie detectors may be used against suspected criminals in court. In other countries, polygraph results, which can be inaccurate, may not be used as evidence.

❮ People taking lie detector tests answer yes-or-no questions while various body functions are monitored.

Digging Deeper

Your Challenge!

Since lie detector tests are not always accurate, some countries do not allow them to be used as evidence. To dig deeper into the issue:

Research the history of polygraph machines. In what circumstances are they most helpful? When do they tend to be least effective? Why?

Summary

Police use polygraph machines to tell whether suspects are lying. However, polygraph results are not always reliable.

Further Inquiry

Even if a suspect can trick a lie detector, there are other ways to link that person to a crime. Maybe we should ask:

How do fingerprints and genetic fingerprinting help solve crimes?

How Do Fingerprints and Genetic Fingerprinting Help Solve Crimes?

Fingerprints are an important tool for solving crimes because no two people have the same prints. Every time a person touches an object, he or she leaves natural oils from the hands on it. The oils are left on the surface in the shape of the person's fingerprint. Even though the fingerprints may be hard to see, their image remains on the object. People began using fingerprints to solve crimes in the 1880s.

Scientists use two methods to collect fingerprints. The first method is to dust areas with a fine powder containing aluminum, a metal that reflects light. This makes fingerprints easier to see and to photograph. Aluminum dusting powder also shows up against both light and dark backgrounds. After dusting, police photograph the prints or lift them off the surface with transparent tape. The second method is to illuminate surfaces with a powerful beam of light called a laser. When the laser lights up an area, it causes fingerprints to glow.

❯ After gathering fingerprints, investigators can look for a match in the database, or online collection, of fingerprints at the Federal Bureau of Investigation.

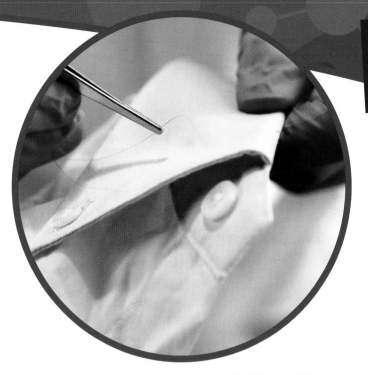

▲ Using saliva, blood, or a strand of hair with a root from the scalp, scientists can identify a suspect with a very high level of certainty.

Some criminals wear gloves to avoid leaving fingerprints. However, they often leave behind hair, blood, or saliva. A thief, for example, may bleed while breaking a window to enter a building. Tiny clues such as these can help police find a criminal.

DNA contains all of the information that makes one living thing different from another. Except for identical twins, every person in the world has different DNA. At many crime scenes, police take samples of all bodily traces. Then, **forensic scientists** test the cell samples with DNA using a special technique that gives a "fingerprint" of a person's DNA. If the genetic fingerprint matches that of a suspect, it is likely that police have found the right person. This method can also help identify dead bodies and prove someone's innocence.

Your Challenge!

Using fingerprints and genetic fingerprinting helps solve crimes. To dig deeper into the issue:

See if you can distinguish fingerprints. Press your fingertip onto a clean mirror. Ask a friend to do the same. Examine each with a magnifying glass. How do they compare?

Summary

Fingerprints are an important tool of investigation. Scientists also analyze the DNA in bodily traces left behind at a crime scene.

Further Inquiry

Fingerprints and genetic fingerprinting help identify suspects as well as victims when necessary. Maybe we should ask:

How do police identify a victim from bones or teeth?

How Do Police Identify a Victim from Bones or Teeth?

Sometimes, the police have only bones left from the victim of a crime. If the teeth are present, experts may compare them with dental records to help identify the person. Otherwise, a **forensic anthropologist** studies the bones to find out information about the victim.

A forensic anthropologist can tell whether bones belong to a man or a woman. Women's bones are often smaller than men's bones. Women also have wider pelvic bones than men. If the person ever broke a bone, the healed break will show. Bones give an idea of how tall a person was. Scientists can also guess an age range from bones. Bones of a very old person look different from the bones of a young person.

❯ Scientists can determine the age of victims by examining their teeth.

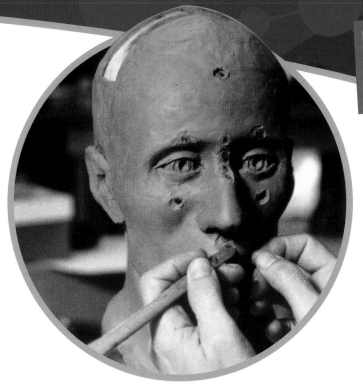

^ Layers of clay can transform a skull into a a kind of sculpture that may be useful for investigators.

Forensic anthropologists use plastic or clay to try to make a face on the victim's skull. This is called facial reconstruction. Scientists know how thick the skin and muscles are on different parts of the face. By building up these areas on the skull, they create faces that look much like that of the people when they were alive. By adding eyes, teeth, and hair, the forensic anthropologist can create faces that may be recognized and identified.

There are slight differences in the size of teeth of each individual. Dental records, which are kept for anyone who has ever been to a dentist, are useful in identifying people. Teeth are not as accurate as fingerprints, because dental records change as a person gets older.

Your Challenge!

Scientists can guess the age of victims by studying their bones. To dig deeper into the issue:

Research how the bones of a young person and of an old person differ. How might investigators tell them apart? What bone features help determine age?

Summary

Bones can tell investigators whether a victim was male or female, old or young, or whether the victim had ever broken a bone. Scientists can also identify a person using dental records.

Further Inquiry

Scientists use facial reconstruction to help identify victims. Maybe we should ask:

How do artists help police solve crimes?

How Do Artists Help Police Solve Crimes?

Witnesses to a crime have seen the suspect, and they know what that person looks like. When this happens, the witness describes the suspect to a police artist. Using the description, the police artist either draws the face on paper or creates a face with a computer program. The artist emphasizes any unique features, such as a large nose or buckteeth. The resulting picture is called a composite. The witness asks for changes to be made until the composite looks like the suspect.

Once a composite is complete, police show the picture to anyone who might recognize the face. Sometimes, composites are printed on posters that describe the crime or shown on television or web pages. Police then ask anyone who recognizes the face to contact them.

> Police sketches have helped bring many criminals to justice.

If someone is a witness to a crime and the police have a suspect, they may show the witness several pictures of people who look similar to the suspect. They also include a photograph of the suspect. If the witness chooses the suspect, it helps to confirm that the police have the right person in custody.

⌄ Police lineups, which typically include five or six people, may or may not include the suspect.

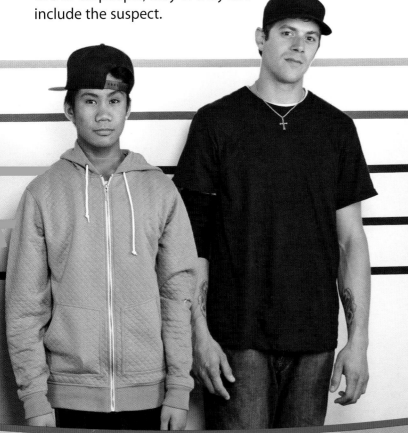

Digging Deeper

Your Challenge!

Police artists create a drawing of a suspect based on descriptions from witnesses. To dig deeper into the issue:

Brainstorm which features of a person's face a witness might be most likely to remember and why. Which ones might be most helpful in creating a composite?

Summary

Witnesses give police artists descriptions of a suspect. Police artists use those descriptions to create a composite. Police publicize the composite to help find the suspect.

Further Inquiry

Witnesses can help identify a subject, but sometimes police have to solve a crime that does not have any witnesses. Maybe we should ask:

What is a profiler?

What Is a Profiler?

Sometimes, police have evidence of a crime, but they may not have any good leads as to who committed the crime. If the crime is a serious one, such as murder, the police ask for help from a profiler. Profilers are **psychologists** who study how criminal minds work.

A profiler studies all the details of a crime to establish what type of person the killer is. The profiler tries to understand why the criminal has committed such a crime. Profilers might determine the gender, age, job, and habits of the criminal. The details that the profiler gives to police are compared to descriptions of anyone connected with the crime. If the description fits someone, that person is questioned.

When police suspect that one person has committed many crimes, they sometimes work with a specialist called a geographic profiler. This person uses information about the locations of the crimes. A geographic profiler can determine where the person who committed the crimes most likely lives. The profiler may also be able to predict the area in which the criminal will strike next.

❯ Mapping the locations of related crimes can narrow down the list of suspects.

Your Challenge!

Police use a geographic profiler when they suspect one person has committed a series of crimes. To dig deeper into the issue:

Do research using online news sources. Make a list of several real-life crimes that were solved with the help of a profiler.

Summary

A profiler uses details of a crime to learn more about the criminal, such as his or her age and habits. That information can help police identify a suspect.

Further Inquiry

Profiling is one way police narrow down suspects. Other clues about a suspect, including the way he or she talks, may also help. Maybe we should ask:

What are voiceprints?

What Are Voiceprints?

Each person has a unique way of speaking. Like fingerprints, speech habits are different from person to person. Even if a person tries to disguise his or her voice, that person will have the same speech patterns.

In certain crimes, police sometimes have a recording of voices as evidence. Recordings of telephone calls may include bomb threats or ransom demands. Scientists listen to different voice recordings to figure out whether they come from the same person.

To compare voices, scientists take two sample recordings and analyze them with a sound spectrograph. This machine creates a voiceprint of each of the recorded voices. Scientists then examine the voiceprints for similarities or use computer software to compare them.

❭ Voiceprints are graphs made of recorded voice sounds.

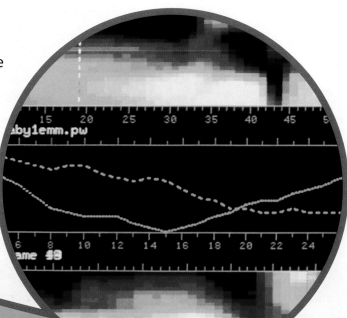

Some companies use voiceprints to help keep buildings safe. In order to enter a building, a person must provide a voiceprint that matches one in the building's voice identification system. The person is then permitted entry.

Your Challenge!

People use specific speech patterns even when they disguise their voices. To dig deeper into the issue:

Experiment to see whether you can identify disguised voices. With a partner, record your normal voices and disguised voices saying the same sentence or phrase. Then play back the recordings and see whether you can identify the voices.

Summary

The voice pattern of every person is unique. Scientists analyze voice recordings with a sound spectograph to create a voiceprint of the sounds.

Further Inquiry

A voiceprint can be used to help prove a suspect's guilt. Blood samples can do the same. Maybe we should ask:

What are blood types?

What Are Blood Types?

Genetic fingerprinting is useful in helping prove a suspect's guilt or innocence. However, testing DNA takes a great deal of time and can be very expensive. Before doing genetic fingerprinting, police usually check the type of blood found at a crime scene and the blood type of the victim and suspects.

Scientists can look at many different parts of blood cells to determine blood type. One way to distinguish between different types of blood is to use the ABO system. In this system, human blood is divided into four types. They are types A, B, AB, and O. Each person's blood is one of these types.

Millions of people in the world have the same blood types, so the ABO system is not always useful in a criminal investigation. Some blood types are less common than others, however, which can help narrow down a group of suspects. If two people have the same blood type, there are other chemicals in the blood that may help scientists tell from whom the blood sample came.

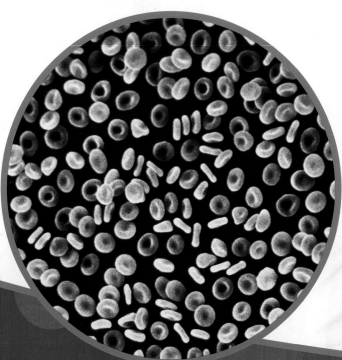

❯ Red blood cells carry oxygen around the body.

Digging Deeper

Your Challenge!

Scientists help police identify the type of blood samples found at the crime scene to see whether it might belong to the victim or suspect. To dig deeper into the issue:

Research the different blood types. Which is most common and which is rarest?

Summary

Police test blood at a crime scene before doing genetic testing. This information might help narrow the group of suspects.

Further Inquiry

Science helps police solve crimes. It can also help prevent them. Maybe we should ask:

How do burglar alarms work?

∧ Scientists determine blood type by examining the surface of red blood cells.

How Do Burglar Alarms Work?

Burglar alarms can help prevent thieves from breaking into homes, offices, and other buildings. A burglar alarm system uses **sensors** to tell if a person has entered the building. The person must show they have permission to enter, by typing a code or using a key, or an alarm will sound.

Burglaries in the 10 Largest U.S. Cities

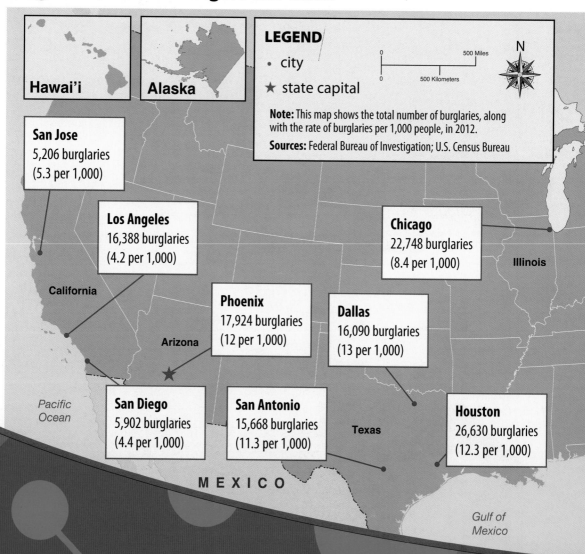

LEGEND
- city
- ★ state capital

Note: This map shows the total number of burglaries, along with the rate of burglaries per 1,000 people, in 2012.

Sources: Federal Bureau of Investigation; U.S. Census Bureau

Hawai'i

Alaska

San Jose
5,206 burglaries
(5.3 per 1,000)

Los Angeles
16,388 burglaries
(4.2 per 1,000)

Chicago
22,748 burglaries
(8.4 per 1,000)

Illinois

California

Phoenix
17,924 burglaries
(12 per 1,000)

Dallas
16,090 burglaries
(13 per 1,000)

Arizona

Pacific
Ocean

San Diego
5,902 burglaries
(4.4 per 1,000)

San Antonio
15,668 burglaries
(11.3 per 1,000)

Texas

Houston
26,630 burglaries
(12.3 per 1,000)

MEXICO

Gulf of Mexico

Burglar alarms often work by producing loud noises that scare away intruders. Some alarm systems connect directly to the police or to a security company. These alarms may or may not make a noise. When this type of alarm goes off, the police or security officers go immediately to the building to see what has happened.

There are two main types of burglar alarms. They are magnetic and infrared alarms.

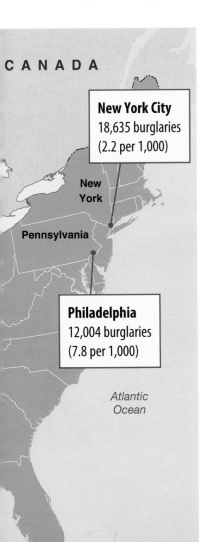

New York City
18,635 burglaries
(2.2 per 1,000)

New York

Pennsylvania

Philadelphia
12,004 burglaries
(7.8 per 1,000)

Atlantic Ocean

CANADA

Magnetic burglar alarms use sensors placed on each window and door of a building. The sensors consist of two parts held together by sealed magnets. If someone opens one of the doors or windows, the two parts of the sensor separate. That sends a signal to the system, which sets off the alarm.

Infrared burglar alarms can sense movement within a building. They sense heat, or infrared radiation, which is given off by people and animals. People cannot see heat energy, but infrared sensors can detect it. The sensors even work in the dark. If the sensors detect any movement, an alarm goes off.

Digging Deeper

Your Challenge!

Some burglar alarms make noise when a person enters a building. To dig deeper into the issue:

Make your own burglar alarm by filling some empty cans with small pebbles. Use string to hang the cans across the place you want to keep safe. You can also set up a stack of cans or bottles so that, if the door is opened, they fall down and make a noise.

Summary

Burglar alarms detect when people enter buildings. Some use magnetic sensors to detect intruders. Others sense body heat.

Further Inquiry

Burglar alarms use technology to prevent crimes. Maybe we should ask:

How do computers help solve crimes?

How Do Computers Help Solve Crimes?

Computers are important tools in the fight against crime. Investigators use them to store large amounts of information. They also use computers to search and retrieve information quickly and easily.

At one time, all information was recorded on paper and kept in files. Using this storage method meant spending a long time to find one specific file. It is much faster to search for information on a computer. Finding information quickly is important to police investigators. Computers assist police by storing large numbers of records and different types of records.

Many investigating organizations keep computer databases that contain information about people's DNA and fingerprints. This information is easy for police to find and may greatly speed up investigations. For example, if a fingerprint is found at a crime scene, a computer quickly compares it to the thousands of fingerprints on record. If the computer locates a match, the police may have found their suspect.

> Digital scanners are used to record fingerprints.

▲ Police officers have laptop computers mounted in their patrol cars to access databases, enter information, and record witness statements at the crime scene.

Before computers, police had to search by hand. Police spent hundreds of hours trying to match a fingerprint from a crime scene with the thousands of fingerprints on record. Computers now conduct searches in just a few minutes.

Computers help police in other ways as well. Using computers, police can find addresses, owners of vehicles, and even photos of criminals in seconds. Police can quickly exchange information with other agencies around the world. Some computer programs can predict what a missing person might look like after several years. Altering an image in this way is called age progression. Police can use that altered image to help find the missing person.

Your Challenge!

Computers make solving crimes faster and more efficient. To dig deeper into the issue:

Research how computers help police solve decades-old crimes. In what ways might other modern advances help solve old cases?

Summary

Computers help police solve crimes by storing large amounts of information, including fingerprints. Police can quickly search through thousands of records in just minutes.

Further Inquiry

Fully understanding crime has involved asking many questions and researching many issues. Taking all we have learned, maybe we finally can answer:

What is a crime?

Putting It All Together

A crime is any action that is against the law. Crimes take place in every country in the world. They range from minor violations such as parking in front of a bus stop to more serious offenses such as burglary and murder. Police search crime scenes for evidence. They carefully photograph and preserve any clues. They identify victims and interview witnesses.

Where Science Fits In

Scientists work hand in hand with police to identify and catch suspects. They use modern technology to uncover secrets hidden in evidence found at crime scenes. Scientists study bullets to determine from what gun they were fired. They perform experiments to learn how and when a victim died. Blood, fingerprints, hair, clothing, and even dirt help connect suspects to crimes. By analyzing DNA left behind at a crime scene, scientists can help police prove a person's guilt or innocence.

Science and the process of scientific inquiry allow us to study and understand crime. They help us recognize how and why crimes occur and what can be done to solve and prevent them. The more we learn about how crimes take place, the more questions police, scientists, and other experts must work to answer.

Careful investigators at the crime scene paired with scientific advances have helped police put criminals behind bars.

Crime-Fighting Careers

Law Enforcement Officers

Police officer and detective are two important jobs in law enforcement. A police officer's biggest tasks are to protect people and find criminals. Some officers patrol their areas on foot, on bicycles, on horseback, or in vehicles to make sure that no crimes are being committed. They also respond to emergency helpline calls. Detectives identify victims and catch people who commit crimes. They look for evidence, interview witnesses and suspects, and make arrests.

Forensic Scientists

Forensic scientists use technology to examine physical evidence found during criminal investigations. They usually work in police laboratories. There are many different types of forensic scientists. Forensic pathologists are doctors who examine bodies to find out how and when death occurred. Forensic anthropologists specialize in studying bones found at crime scenes. Forensic biologists study body fluids, such a blood or saliva. DNA specialists are experts in studying genetic material. Forensic entomologists study insects found at crime scenes.

Young Scientists at Work

Fingerprinting is a valuable tool for police trying to identify a suspect. How does this fingerprint activity show your ability to detect crimes?

Materials

Ink pad

White paper

Drinking glass

Dusting powder (cocoa or chocolate powder)

Paintbrush

Clear tape

Instructions

1. Ask several family members or friends to let you fingerprint them. Press each person's pointer finger firmly on the ink pad and then on the piece of paper. Label each print with the name of the person.

2. Ask the group to choose one of the fingerprinted people to put his or her fingerprints on a drinking glass. Be sure they do not tell you which person touched the glass. Gently brush some dusting powder onto the object with the paintbrush.

3. If you uncover a fingerprint, press a piece of clear tape gently but firmly over the print.

4. Carefully remove the tape, and stick it on the white paper.

Observations

Compare the print to the ones you collected earlier. Can you figure out which person the print belongs to? See if you can find and identify fingerprints on other items around your home.

Quiz

How much do you know about things you and your family can do to stay safe at home? Safety steps include posting a list of phone numbers to call in an emergency and checking that smoke detectors work. There are several other tips to help you and your family live more safely.

How can you stay safe online? Never give personal information on a public website without a parent's permission. You should not share your full name, age, birth date, telephone number, or address.

What should you say if you answer the telephone? Never tell the person calling that you are home alone. It is better to say, "My parent is busy right now. Can I take a message?"

Do you know what to do in an emergency? If there is a fire, serious injury, or other emergency in your home, call 9-1-1. Be prepared to give details and your address.

Do your doors and window lock properly? If not, tell a parent. Be sure to close and lock doors when you go out and after you come home.

Key Words

bacteria: a group of tiny one-celled organisms

cells: the smallest structures that make up all living things

DNA: deoxyribonucleic acid, which is found in most cells of every living organism

evidence: any clues or details that may help investigators solve a crime

forensic anthropologist: a person who studies bones for information about a person

forensic pathologists: people who use medical knowledge for legal purposes

forensic scientists: people who work in any science that helps investigators find and analyze evidence that can be used in a court of law

forgers: people who make or alter a document or object to deceive others

fungi: types of plants without leaves, flowers, or roots

genetic material: chemicals in a cell that determine the traits passed from parents to offspring

holograms: images made by laser beams that look three-dimensional

larvae: insects at the wormlike stage of development between egg and pupa

organism: a living thing

pollen: tiny grains, often yellow, that are produced in flowers

psychologists: people who specialize in studying the mind and human behavior

ransom: the amount of money that is demanded or paid to free a person being held captive

sensors: pieces of equipment that respond to a particular type of change in the environment

traits: qualities that help distinguish people or things from one another

will: a legal document that states what to do with a person's property after that person's death

Index

Log on to www.av2books.com

AV[2] by Weigl brings you media enhanced books that support active learning. Go to www.av2books.com, and enter the special code found on page 2 of this book. You will gain access to enriched and enhanced content that supplements and complements this book. Content includes video, audio, weblinks, quizzes, a slide show, and activities.

AV[2] Online Navigation

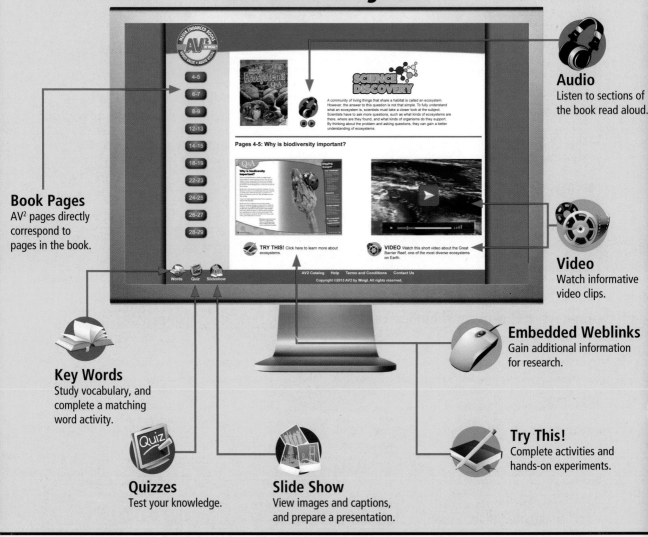

Audio
Listen to sections of the book read aloud.

Book Pages
AV[2] pages directly correspond to pages in the book.

Video
Watch informative video clips.

Embedded Weblinks
Gain additional information for research.

Key Words
Study vocabulary, and complete a matching word activity.

Try This!
Complete activities and hands-on experiments.

Quizzes
Test your knowledge.

Slide Show
View images and captions, and prepare a presentation.

AV[2] was built to bridge the gap between print and digital. We encourage you to tell us what you like and what you want to see in the future.

Sign up to be an AV[2] Ambassador at www.av2books.com/ambassador.